Agents of Christ: The Prodigal Daughter: A Christian Novel

Christian Youth Faith-Walkers Series

C.Orville McLeish

Published by HCP Book Publishing, 2024.

While every precaution has been taken in the preparation of this book, the publisher assumes no responsibility for errors or omissions, or for damages resulting from the use of the information contained herein.

AGENTS OF CHRIST: THE PRODIGAL DAUGHTER: A CHRISTIAN NOVEL

First edition. July 7, 2024.

Copyright © 2024 C.Orville McLeish.

ISBN: 979-8227193421

Written by C.Orville McLeish.

Also by C.Orville McLeish

Christian Youth Faith-Walkers Series
Detour: A Christian Novel
The Preacha And The Prostitute: A Christian Novel
Agents of Christ: The Prodigal Daughter: A Christian Novel

The Unshakable Series
FAITH: A Theological Memoir

Standalone
Girl Unknown
Who I Am In Christ Daily Devotionals
How to Receive Your Healing
Sons of God: A Study on the Biblical Narrative of the Sons of
God
Made in God's Image: We are Partakers of God's Divine Nature

Watch for more at https://clevelandomcleish.com/.

To all young orphans and those who have lost a parent:
God has not abandoned you.

Chapter 1

Allan Johnson looked out over his new neighborhood. He had a nice three bedroom, two bath ranch, surrounded by tall, strong trees. He felt strong, almost human, sitting among the branches of the oak tree. He plucked a leaf from the branch on which he sat and inspected it.

Being given a house meant he'd be getting his first assignment soon. He pressed the leaf to his nose and inhaled. Becoming a full-fledged Agent of Christ was so close he could smell it. It was almost as real as this fresh green leaf.

Life on Earth was so thrilling. He closed his eyes and enjoyed the aroma of life.

"Why are you sniffing that leaf like that?" said a male's voice nearby.

He knew the voice. It was one of his AOC colleagues, Agent Kaliel.

Allan opened his eyes and, as expected, saw no one. All the same, he knew Kaliel was there. And, if Kaliel was nearby, so was Martin.

Why they preferred to remain invisible, even to other Agents, was a mystery to him. Surely they had their reasons, but he had to admit it was an odd habit. He wondered, though, when he was an Agent for as long as them if he would stop making himself visible too.

He shrugged the thought off and decided to play along.

"Hello, Kaliel," Allan said, "And, morning greetings to you as well Martin."

Martin cleared his throat and huffed. "Man, I was going to push you off that branch before you noticed me."

Allan chuckled. "You two always travel together. Like salt and pepper, or ketchup and mustard."

"No, we don't," Martin instantly protested.

"Never mind," Kaliel said as he made himself visible. "We came to give you the good news."

Allan's eyes widened. "My first assignment starts today?"

Martin appeared and was wagging his head sadly. "No, my friend. Soon, though. Very soon. You have a house now, situated in a neighborhood, with many troubled humans." He frowned as he cast his eye over the neighboring houses. "Too many for my blood."

"I'm here to serve," Allan countered. "I don't mind living among them, helping them through their difficulties. It's what I was trained for. Soon, you say. How soon?"

Kaliel and Martin looked at each other and laughed. Allan brushed their teasing off.

"You used to be like that, Kaliel. You did," Martin said.

Kaliel's smile evaporated. "No, I wasn't."

"Yeah, you were," Martin insisted. "Eager Beaver. That's what they called you back at the Academy. Ole Eager Beaver."

"Nothing wrong with being eager," Kaliel said. "Right, Allan?"

Allan nodded. Being eager had gotten him to the top of his recruiting class and had earned him a spot in the field, more than a year before most of his classmates.

"So, if today is not the day that I get my first assignment, why are you here?"

Martin cleared his throat again and pulled a small white box out of his pocket. He gave Kaliel a questioning look, then handed the box to Allan.

"What's this?" Allan asked.

"We came to deliver the newly upgraded equipment you were promised," Martin said. "Go on, open it."

Inside, Allan found what looked like a smart phone.

"You know what that is, right?" Kaliel asked.

"Of course I do. It's my communicator. I graduated top of my class. I'm familiar with all the equipment."

Kaliel scoffed. "That doesn't mean anything."

"Hey," Martin protested. "Anyway, that particular model of communicator is single use. Not like the one you were trained with. You're the first to use it in the field. It's only for extreme emergencies. Use it only if you need to call in reinforcements."

Allan nodded. He felt like levitating right then and flying straight to the moon. He had his own AOC communicator. And, the newest model at that.

Woohoo!

Kaliel must have noticed Allan's excitement because he placed his hand on his arm. "Calm down, Sparky. This isn't a toy, you know."

"I know." Allan took a calming breath. "I thought I also got a vision cube."

"Well, you don't get a vision cube," he responded as he lifted the communicator out of the box. Allan saw a silver rectangle about the size of a credit card at the bottom of the box.

He let out a low whistle. Was that what he thought it was?

"This is a vision *card*, isn't it?" Allan asked. He could feel his heart racing.

"Sparky," Kaliel said, his face grave. "I'm not sure you're ready for being in the field. This isn't a game, Agent Johnson."

"I know that. I am so ready."

"You're shaking like a leaf."

"I'm just extremely excited."

"Excitement is one thing. Being a nervous wreck is quite another thing. Get a hold of yourself, Agent Johnson."

Allan took a few deep breaths and tried to appear calmer. Inside, his heart still raced with excitement. "I'm not nervous. I assure you."

Kaliel and Martin did not look convinced.

"We're dealing with a person's life here," Martin said, the frown on his face deepening. "You're an Agent of Christ. Not Denzel Washington in *Preacher's Wife*."

Preacher's Wife?

"I know. I really and truly do know," Allan said.

Martin continued, not looking convinced. "You have no room for error. They are depending on us to minister to them in times of distress and discomfort. To rescue them in times of trouble."

Kaliel joined Martin's speech. "Indeed. When they cry out to God for help. He sends us. At a moment's notice."

"In less than a blink of an eye," Martin interrupted.

"We are to come to their assistance," Kaliel followed. "There is no time to catch your breath, or to calm your nerves."

Martin nodded in agreement. "An Agent of Christ in the field is level-headed, always. Always."

The two senior agents looked Allan in the eye.

"Are you level-headed, Johnson?" Kaliel asked him.

"Many Agents of Christ," Martin shared, "have been lured away by the lusts and vanities of this world. Some of our former agents have allowed themselves, in moments of great weakness and even excitement, to be drawn to the Dark Side."

Kaliel continued, "Special Agents, like Martin and I, are on a mission to identify and eliminate those rogue agents. They must be removed quickly and completely, and bound forever in Outer Darkness. We don't want to have to remove you from this realm, and escort you to the Darkness for all eternity because you have allowed yourself to be drawn away from your mission."

Allan squared his shoulders. He now felt the gravity of the situation. They were right. This was not a game or an exciting 'project'. What he was about to embark on was life changing for a real person. Not just for him.

And he surely did not want to be known for straying, for going "dark."

"I understand," he said and looked at both of them before continuing. "I was letting my sense of adventure get the best of me. I was serious when I pledged before our Commander to not let pride or lust betray my devotion to the Son of Light and Love. And, I am serious now. Thank you for reminding me of the oath I took."

His peers smiled back at him. "Good, Young Blood," Kaliel said, taking the vision card from Allan. "Let me continue telling you about the vision card. As you can see, it's no bigger than a credit card, but it is extremely powerful. If you thought the vision cubes you used in training were wonderful, then these babies will blow you away."

Martin took Allan's hand and turned it palm up. Kaliel placed the card in the middle of Allan's palm. The surface of the card changed from silver to black, to sky blue within mere seconds. "Watch carefully," Martin said. "The card shows the future. Things that are about to happen that is. But only the future of your primary assignment who is, in this case, a woman."

A woman?

Allan couldn't help but frown. Why was he being assigned to a woman? He knew that sometimes they did do cross-gender assignments, but he had hoped that he would be assigned to a man. He had heard they gave you less drama.

Oh well. Can't win them all, he thought.

Martin went on. "The card works a lot like the vision cube. The vision will play across the card for a short period. The difference with the card is this: the vision will only appear when someone of true faith is praying for the human you have been assigned to serve. The Prodigal Daughter."

"The Prodigal Daughter," Allan repeated softly.

Allan saw what appeared to be a small video playing on the surface of the card. There was a woman talking to a man. The couple appeared to be in a kitchen. She seemed to be agitated about something. She pulled snapshots from an envelope and threw them on the table strewn with Cheerios and spilled milk. The photos scattered everywhere.

Allan heard the woman yell, "Why do you have these pictures of young girls in your underwear drawer, Vance?"

The man shook his head and cursed at her. "Why are you in my underwear drawer, woman?" he shouted.

"You're my husband. My *husband*, Vance. I thought we agreed that we would not keep secrets. Is this your little secret? Getting it on with little girls? This is nasty!"

"Leave me alone!"

The man cursed again at the woman and pushed her aside before storming out of the room.

The woman pursued him. "Some of these girls are naked, Vance. Naked."

The scene on the card went away as quickly as it appeared.

Kaliel released a long sigh. "Deeply troubling things are going on in this very neighborhood, Agent Johnson."

He and Martin looked out over the idyllic neighborhood. Allan looked too, though this time, instead of seeing only goodness, he realized that trouble lurked just beneath the surface.

"There is a great need for my service here," he said.

Martin nodded. "Yes, Johnson. The need is great. I'm glad you see that now. I'm glad you see that."

"Are you ready for your first assignment, Sparky?" Kaliel asked.

Allan nodded. "Yes. I am."

Chapter 2

Agent Allan Johnson did not have to wait long to get his assignment. The golden envelope containing the details was delivered at 7 AM sharp.

The Prodigal Daughter's name was Kerrian Croft and she lived at 49 Oak Avenue, right across the street from him.

At 7:15 AM, the scene that he had witnessed on the vision card had started in real life. He could not see it as clearly, but he could hear it through the walls of their house.

Invisible to the world, he was standing on their front lawn, looking through the couple's front windows.

Within seconds, the front door sprang open. Vance, the husband, marched for the car. He had a gym bag in his hand and a scowl on his face. Once he was behind the wheel of his car, he rammed it in reverse and peeled off down the street, narrowly missing an oncoming car.

That car careened into Kerrian Croft's driveway and a woman got out.

"That would be Lisa Henderson, Kerrian's younger sister," Allan whispered to himself.

Allan had memorized all of Lisa's information from the envelope. The analytical side of him wanted to repeat all the data, but the compassionate side could not allow that.

He watched in pain as the sisters embraced on Kerrian's front step.

"Thank you for coming, Lisa," Kerrian said before stepping out of her sister's embrace. "But you can go back home now."

"You ain't pushing me away this time, girl. What happened?"

"We had a fight."

"Well, that much is obvious. The man almost ran me over just now."

"He says he won't be coming back. I really don't want to talk about this now."

"Listen, I know you and I know your husband. You two are smart people. You can work out your differences."

"Yeah, right. Smart people. Did you know my husband has an obsessive crush on little girls? He has pictures of them."

Lisa matched her sister's look of disgust. "What? Oh my God. But surely he can get help. You can get a counselor."

"Leave me alone, please. I'm sorry I called you." Kerrian turns to go back into her house. "I can handle this on my own. I'm a big girl."

"I see the writing on the wall, Kerry."

Kerrian faced her sister and crossed her arms. "And what does that mean?"

"That you're going to run again. You're good at running away. When times get tough or something doesn't go your way. Instead of staying and working it out, you run."

"What? Listen, Lisa. I don't need this sermon. Just cause you go to church does not make you any better than me."

Allan's mind revisited the data he had filed away in his memory. Lisa went to the same church he visited the last two Sundays. He had to admit that he had noticed the pretty young woman and seen the trouble on her face. She seemed to know many of the regulars but kept to herself. It was almost as if she was going to church out of guilt instead of pleasure.

But of course back then, he did not know that she would be part of his assignment, although indirectly.

Kerrian turned toward the door again. "I've got this under control. As you can see, my dog of a husband is gone and I'm fine."

"Kerry, let me stay a few days. I have a suitcase in my car. I want to make sure he doesn't come back and hurt you like he did last time you had a fight."

Kerrian looked over her shoulder. She shrugged like she didn't really care if her sister stayed or not. But, Allan knew differently. The pictures of her face and arms after her last fight with her husband broke Allan's heart.

"Suit yourself," Kerrian said. "The guest bedroom is all yours."

Allan waited until Lisa retrieved her bag, went into the house, and locked the door behind her before he made himself visible.

In his hand, he held an empty measuring cup. He plastered on a smile and rang the doorbell.

Lisa answered the door. "Hello. Can I help you?"

She eyed the measuring cup in his hand.

Allan smiled wider. He hoped this worked. "I ... uh ... I was wondering if I could borrow a cup or two of flour."

Lisa was smiling back but had a look of doubt in her eyes. "Well, which is it? One cup or two cups?"

"Uh ... Two?"

She chuckled. "You don't cook much do you?"

Kerrian called to her sister from another room, "Who is it? I don't want to buy anything from a salesman."

"Not a salesman. One of your neighbors, I think." Lisa squinted at him. "But, you do look familiar. I think I've seen you before."

Kerrian joined her sister at the door and looked at Allan from head to toe. Allan felt like a piece of clothing on the rack. "Hello, neighbor. I've seen you working in your yard, trying to climb that big tree. What's your name?"

"Where are your manners, Kerrian," Lisa scolded her.

"Where are *my* manners? What about his? Has he introduced himself yet?"

Allan blushed. "Pardon me. I'm so sorry. I was so focused on my measuring cup. My name is Allan Johnson."

The two sisters shook his hand. Lisa's handshake and smile was the warmer of the two.

"Come in," Lisa said.

"You just met the man, and now you're inviting him into *my* house?"

"You said he was your neighbor."

Kerrian rolled her eyes and left Lisa and Allan standing on the doorstep.

"Please excuse my sister, Allan. She's had a recent shock." Lisa stepped aside. "Please come in. I'll see about giving you a cup or *two* of sugar."

"Flour, not sugar," Allan corrected.

"Sorry. Flour." She winked at him. Was she privy to his ploy? He wondered.

Allan followed her to the kitchen and stood quietly as she filled the measuring cup to the brim.

"There, that should hold you for a little while."

"Thank you," he said and turned to leave.

Thankfully she stopped him with an offer for coffee.

Inwardly, he smiled. "Yes, I would love a cup."

"Well, take a seat and I'll brew up something good." She pulled a coffee pot out of the cabinet. "Secretly, I'm hoping that the smell of coffee will draw my sister out of her room."

Allan nodded. He could hear a TV playing in another part of the house. It sounded far away. "Kerrian seems so sad. I hope the coffee works."

Lisa nodded. "Sad ain't the half of it. But, usually good coffee and good company brings her around." She suddenly snapped her fingers and pointed at Allan. "That's where I know you from. The coffee bar at church. You've been there for the past couple Sundays, talking to old Mrs. Blackburn."

Allan laughed. She was quite a talker.

"That woman can talk."

"Don't I know it?" They laughed. "But, she's so lonely. All she has is her little terrier at home. I don't mind her talking my ear off one bit."

Lisa laughed again. "Oh, she'll talk both ears off if you let her."

Over the next hour, Lisa reacted to his comments as he predicted. She talked and talked. She was chattier than the old lady from church.

The information she shared wasn't news to him. He knew it all from the vision card, or from the files, but hearing her speak them was important. The files did not show the sadness she felt seeing her sister suffer in a bad marriage. Neither did it show the sense of betrayal and distrust she still felt about being abandoned by her mother at an early age.

Allan smiled to himself. This assignment was going to be so easy. Open and shut, he thought, then he remembered that Lisa was not the Prodigal Daughter. Her sister was.

And in the hour he spent in the house that day, Lisa's sister never showed her face again.

Chapter 3

Four days later, he found himself on Kerrian's doorstep again. Lisa's smiling face appeared on the other side of the opened door.

"Hey."

"Hey, Allan. Come on in."

Allan stepped past her and she closed the door. "How is she?" he asked, referring to Kerrian.

"Hard to say. She's taken off a few days from work. Each morning she gets up and goes jogging. She hangs at the gym for hours and hours. Then comes back in the afternoon, takes a shower, goes to sleep. Then she wakes up in the night to watch television and falls asleep on the couch. Then, she starts over again the next day."

"Sounds normal. Like she's trying to spring back from the shock of breaking up with Vance. Like she's trying to get her head on straight."

Allan hoped he was using the right slang. Lisa just kept talking.

"Well, sooner or later she'll need a reality check. Life goes on. She's changed the locks on the house, thank goodness. And, I don't think her husband Vance has called her but I'm still worried."

"God has a way of working it out."

"He better do it fast. I think something's going on in her mind that we don't know about. She needs counseling."

"Do you think she'll run away again?"

Lisa nodded. "That's how she deals with problems, Allan. This house and this neighborhood will constantly remind her of the pain. Sooner or later, Kerrian is going to start running again."

He shook his head. "Any word on your mother?"

Lisa pulled a newspaper from under the couch and handed it to Allan, pointing at a certain section. "I placed an ad in the paper like you said. I got two calls claiming to be cousins, but I haven't followed up on that yet. I don't know if I should."

"Why not?"

"Because I don't trust people. They can very deceitful."

"Well, that's true, but these are leads. We should follow up. I still think her mother will be the key to her redemption."

"If you say so."

"You don't believe?"

"I'm willing to try anything once, just to see my sister smile again."

"Well, that will have to do for now. In time, you'll believe." He smiled.

"We'll see. Anyway, I think she may have seen the ad but I'm not sure yet."

Allan was confused. "Your mother?"

"No, silly. Kerrian."

Allan signed with relief. "Oh. Okay."

"I saw her staring at the paper for a while, then she threw it down. I hid it just in case she had second thoughts and wanted to see it again."

"The ad is pretty clever. You said a whole lot without saying anything much."

"I'm a journalist remember. I have my skills."

Allan smiled approvingly. Lisa was a talented writer but before he could tell her so, the front door opened. He heard Kerrian speaking and laughing with someone. He knew who it was.

Instantly, his mind went back to the scene he had seen from the vision card just hours before coming over. The vision was the reason why he had come over. Because the man he saw with Kerrian was not her husband but a former Agent of Christ that called himself Jason Jones among the humans. He had gone rogue months earlier but had not been captured.

Allan slipped his hand into the pocket of his jeans and touched his communicator. Would he be using it today? Would he need to call in Martin and K? Why hadn't they captured Jason yet? He hadn't seen his senior agents since their conversation in the tree. Had they been pulled away on another case?

From his training, he knew that before a rogue agent could be bound in Outer Darkness, a certain body of appropriate evidence had to be gathered. Allan hated that rule. In his book, if an agent went dark, they needed to be zapped with lightning right away. They should not be allowed to roam the Earth, searching for humans to devour.

As Lisa hid the newspaper, Kerrian turned the corner into the living room where they sat. The man that had entered with Kerrian stood back several feet. He wore workout clothes and stood there looking innocent.

Allan wanted to knock that friendly smirk off his face.

Lisa smiled and greeted Kerrian. "My favorite sister. Give me a hug!"

"No," Kerrian protested. "No hug. Just came from the gym."

"Too late," Lisa sang out and wrapped her sister in a tight hug. "I missed you."

"I've only been gone a couple hours."

"Really?" Lisa flashed Jason a smile. "I see you brought home something for a change."

Kerrian cleared her throat. "Lisa and Allan, this is Jason. I met him at the gym a few days ago. He's one of the trainers."

Trainer, my foot.

Allan narrowed his eyes at the man as he shook Lisa's hand and smiled.

Kerrian giggled and took Jason by the forearm. "Jason kept insisting that I bring him to see my home gym. I think he's trying to convince me that I need a personal trainer and pay his expensive fees."

Jason chuckled. "I'm doing nothing of the sort. I just want to make sure you are doing the correct exercises in the correct way. Besides, my fees aren't that high. The first two sessions are free."

He winked at Lisa.

"Um. Okay," Lisa said. "Well, this is Allan Johnson. One of Kerry's neighbors and he goes to my church. You remember that red and white checkered building down the road with the big cross at the top. They have a nice marriage ministry that you and Vance used to go to."

Kerrian frowned at her sister. "Very funny, sis. So you two dating or something, Allan? I've seen you more since my sister came to visit than I've ever seen you."

Allan and Lisa answered together. "No!"

Then Lisa added. "He's a good friend."

Kerrian pursed her lips and said, "I see."

While the sisters sparred verbally, Allan stared at Jason.

"What, something in my teeth?" Jason asked him.

"Nothing at all," Allan said with a fake smile.

Kerrian rubbed her midsection and headed for the kitchen. "What's for dinner? I'm hungry."

"Sorry, sis. I didn't get a chance to cook. Even though I've been working remotely these past few days, I have been very busy."

"You could order out," Jason suggested.

Allan glared at him.

"Or not," Jason said.

"No, Jason," Kerrian interrupted. "That's a good idea. Then, after we eat, I can take you to the basement and look at my workout setup. Let's order some Chinese food. I have a friend who works at the restaurant two blocks from here."

Dinner went as well as Allan expected. Kerrian chatted almost nonstop with Jason while her sister looked uncomfortable.

After they were all full of enough egg rolls, sesame chicken, and fried rice, Jason pushed back from the dining room table and volunteered to help with the dishes.

Lisa sprang to her feet. "Great. I welcome the help. My sister is allergic to doing dishes. This way, sir."

She led him into the next room. Allan heard the rush of water into the sink and the click of dishes and silverware. He decided this was his moment to talk with Kerrian.

He cleared his throat. She looked at him momentarily, then turned her face away.

"You shouldn't stare at a young lady like that. It makes them uncomfortable."

"Oh, sorry. I didn't realize that I was staring."

"Why are you here, Alex?"

"It's Allan."

"Yeah, right. Allan, why are you here?"

"Are you always this direct?"

"Not really. It's a little character trait I picked up recently."

"Oh, I thought it was FDM."

"What's FDM?"

"Feminine defense mechanism. It's something females develop after being in a few bad relationships."

"Oh really. So you're a counselor or something? Did my sister put you up to this? I know she thinks I need counseling. I also know she loves me, but she's overbearing sometimes. She acts like she's the big sister."

"Well, who can dispute the love between two siblings?"

"Are you going to answer the question?"

Allan did not like the response he was getting from Kerrian. She seemed to be getting more closed-minded by the second. How could he draw her out?

Honesty and directness were the key, he figured. No more beating around the bush.

"I have no intimate interest here. I'm not trying to get in bed with your sister. If that's what you're suggesting. I'm just a friend. That's all."

"Right," she said, playing with her paper napkin. "I would believe you considering the fact that you sound very sincere. I appreciate your honesty, but unfortunately, I doubt very much that there is one sincere man left on this god-forsaken planet."

"You can't judge a man because you made a few bad choices."

"Who said I made bad choices?"

The direct answer worked before. He decided to try it again, even though, deep down, it made him feel uncomfortable by putting others on the spot.

"You're still wearing a wedding ring and you're spending time with someone you met in the gym the other day. It's not that hard to tell that you're facing marital issues."

Kerrian looks at the ring on her finger. Her face seemed to soften but then with a flash of her dark brown eyes at him, she hardened again. "Even if I was, it's none of your business."

"Kerrian, I'm trying to be your friend."

"If you must know, I have filed for divorce. Not sure why I'm still wearing this ring." She takes it off and tosses it on the table. "I'm done giving Vance Croft a second chance. You want to know what I think about friendship and men? There is no man alive who wants to be 'just friends' with someone like me. You only have one thing on your mind. That's how you men think. That's the only thing that drives you."

"I'm not like that."

"Tell that to some stupid woman who is yet to learn the true nature of men."

"If you see all men as evil, why are you seeing Jason? Do you trust him?"

"No. And I don't trust you either."

Kerrian got up and left. Allan heard a door slam in another part of the house. Allan sighed. That conversation went poorly. He slumped in his chair.

"This is going to be a whole lot tougher than I thought," he mumbled to himself.

"What'd you say?" Lisa said as she returned to the dining room. She was drying her hands with a flowery dish towel. "Where's Kerrian?"

"I think I made her mad," Allan admitted. "She went to her room, I think."

"What happened?" she asked. Jason stood behind her.

"Bad start," he said.

"Oh boy. Don't worry. I'll take care of it."

She tossed the dish towel on the table and left Allan alone with Jason.

Jason didn't waste any time on small talk with Allan. "I know who you are, Agent Johnson. I know why you're here."

"And I know who you are, former Agent Jones."

Jason let out a sly laugh. In a heartbeat, Allan was in his face, pushing him into the wall.

"Get your hands off me, Johnson."

"I will not allow you to cause this family any more pain."

"So, you're Mr. Hero now. Well, Superman, you're here on a mission and so am I. May the best man win."

Jason shoved Allan aside and left the house. Allan was extremely disturbed.

"This is really not going according to plan," Allan said to himself.

Lisa returned and flopped down in a chair across from Allan. "She seems really upset. She won't let me in. What exactly did you say to her?"

"I just told her I wanted to be her friend and that I wasn't interested in you intimately."

Lisa let her head fall back against the back of the chair. "That's it. Boy, she must really be functioning on low fuel."

"This guy Jason is bad news. I don't think he's up to any good."

"It's a little early for you to be playing jealous boyfriend."

"No, really. Something he said made me think he's up to no good. I don't think it's a good idea for Kerrian to be around this guy."

"Well, I won't be the one to tell her, so be my guest."

"I can't just tell her not to see him."

"You seem to have a way with people, Allan. Give it another try, please." She took a deep breath and stood up. Allan joined her.

"I should probably be getting back to my house," he said.

She checked the clock on the wall. "Oh wow. I have to go too. I'm meeting with one of our 'cousins' in the next half an hour."

"I hope you have a more productive time with them than the one I've with your sister."

"We'll see. Go home and rest. I'll call you tomorrow."

"Okay, Lisa." He started walking toward the front door. "Thanks for dinner."

"You're welcome. Oh, one more thing."

Allan turned around.

"Chocolate," she said, a smile stretched across her face.

"What?"

"Kerrian loves chocolate. That's one way to win her over."

Allan smiled too. "Thanks. Chocolate. I'll keep that in mind."

Chapter 4

Agent Allan Johnson did not like what the vision card was showing him that night. It made him wish all the more that he had punched Jason Jones when he had the chance.

The vision had only lasted three seconds, but it was long enough to see why Jason held so much control over Kerrian. She longed for approval on a deep level. For some reason beyond him, she thought a handsome man like Jason would give her that.

Allan clenched his fists. He had to take action. There had to be some way to intervene. Some way to help Kerrian see that what she really needed was the approval of the ones who had given her life, her mother, and her Creator.

What could he do to help Kerrian see this?

"Dear God, help me think," he muttered.

One word came to him.

Chocolate.

In a flash, Allan had the box of chocolates in one hand and his neighbor's doorknob in his other.

Without thinking, he had turned the knob and stepped into Kerrian's house.

"Who is it?" Kerrian called from somewhere deeper in the house.

"Um ... um ... It's Allan," he stammered.

She stumbled into view, clearly drunk. Tears stained her face. "What do you want? Why are you in my house? I didn't hear the doorbell."

Allan stared at her, dumbfounded. Seeing her in person in this state tore his heart apart. It was worse than what he saw on the vision card.

"Well, what do you want? To see me drinking my sorrows away. Is that box of chocolate for my sister? She's not home."

"I know."

"Then, why are you here?" She staggered into the living room. "No one is ever where you want them to be."

"Would it help to say I'm sorry for the pain you're in?"

"Whatever for? You haven't done anything wrong. Other than being a silly bothersome man."

Allan followed her. "I'm sorry anyway. We got off to a bad start and I was hoping we could start over."

"What exactly do you want, Alex?"

"Allan."

"Whatever."

Allan handed her the box of chocolate. She was reluctant at first but then she snatched it and tore open the packaging like a hungry wolf.

"How did you know I like chocolate? Wait, don't answer that. I think I already know the answer. Thank you, but nothing has changed between us."

Allan was all smiles.

"Tell me something, Allan. Why are men so manipulative? You go to lengths to find out what a woman wants and you give it to her. You tell her all the right things she wants to hear every day. Stir up all her emotions, and then she falls for you simply because you do and say all the right things. Then, you rip her heart to shreds. Why do men do that?"

"I'm not sure."

"Let me be a little more specific so you don't have to speak for all men. Why do you do it?"

"I'm not like that, Kerrian. What you see is what you get?"

"There you go."

"What."

"You're telling me exactly what I want to hear."

"I'm telling the truth."

"There you go again."

"You know, somehow I don't think we're getting anywhere with this conversation."

"You know, I think you're right."

"Kerrian, look, I know how difficult life can sometimes be, but if you just have faith in God."

"God?"

"Yes, the big Man upstairs."

"Do you know him?"

"Yes, I do."

Kerrian threw her head back and laughed. "You almost sound like you do believe in God. Well, the next time you guys talk, ask him why he has been ignoring me all these years."

"I don't think..."

"Ask him why he never answers my prayers. Ask him when will I have a just little bit of peace."

Kerrian's smile turned into a grimace. Fresh tears coursed down her face. She cursed. "Where's my bottle?"

"Don't do this, Kerrian."

She stood up, dropping the box of chocolates. "Ask him why I have to suffer so much and make so many bad choices even when it seems he's the one guiding my decisions. Ask him why he had to make such a huge mess out of my life."

Kerrian lifted her arms heavenward and screamed at the ceiling. "All I want is peace!"

"Stop, please."

"Maybe you can speak highly of God, Allan. Maybe you have some pretty sweet testimony that you give in church every Sunday. But, I have nothing but pain to show for my service to the Almighty."

"We don't usually get what we want in life."

"Stick a pin, right there. I don't even remember asking you for advice. Why are you here, Allan? It seems like every time I see you, all the bitterness, the anger, the hurt, everything just comes up to the surface. I don't think I like you, Allan."

"You have to face these elements in order to overcome your past."

"I am not interested in overcoming anything. I just want to live my life in peace, Allan. Am I asking too much? I want to be free from all this. I want to be free for once in my life. Do you understand what I'm trying to say?"

"I do."

"Then leave me alone, Allan," she shrieked. "I am not interested in friendship anymore. All I want is peace. Do you hear me? Peace!"

Allan felt a dark presence behind him and instantly knew who it was.

"Why are you here, Jason?" Allan asked.

Kerrian came to herself and clapped her hands over her mouth.

Jason chuckled. "Peace? Did I hear you talking about peace, Kerry? What was that all about, sweetheart?"

He stepped around Allan and extended his hands to Kerrian. Kerrian stumbled into Jason's arms.

"Here's your peace, Kerry. Right here in my arms. Come away with me."

Allan saw her head nodding gently against Jason's chest. "Take me away from here, Jason."

"Now?"

"Yes. This very minute."

Jason started to lead Kerrian out of the room. Allan stepped in front of them. "Where are you taking her?"

"That's my business, Superman."

"What if I make it my business, Jason?"

Jason laughed. "She's leaving under her free will. You know the rules. You can't stop me. I'm not making her go. She's choosing to leave."

His face was inches from Allan's face.

Close enough to hit, Allan thought.

He knew Jason was right about the rulebook and he hated him for it.

There was only one way out for Kerrian. She had to change her mind.

"Kerrian," Allan begged. "This isn't a path to peace."

She let her head roll to one side and looked up into Jason's face. "Why are we still here, honey?"

She and Jason walked out of the house leaving the door open. And there was nothing Allan could do to stop them. He felt so useless.

What did an Agent of Christ do when they failed their mission?

He pulled the communicator from his pocket. Was this the time to call Martin and Kaliel?

Lord, help me think!

For the longest time, he stood in the middle of Kerrian's living room, with the floor littered with trampled chocolates, thinking and praying. Wishing for a single glimpse from the vision card.

The faithful one who had been praying for Kerrian had stopped. But why?

"Keep praying. Please," he whispered.

"Who are you talking to, Allan?"

He turned toward the voice behind him and was happy to see Lisa.

A look of concern spread across his face. "Are you okay? You were standing there talking to yourself."

"I'm fine. Just worried about your sister."

"Where is she?"

"She left a while ago with Jason. I think he's taking her somewhere far way. Possibly dangerous."

Lisa frowned. "How do you know that?"

"I just have this bad feeling."

He stooped and started cleaning up the chocolate candy on the floor. Lisa joined him.

"I see you took my advice about the chocolate."

"It backfired, sort of."

Lisa considered him for a second. "Thanks for trying. Well, hopefully, she'll be back soon. I've texted and called her. Allan, you won't believe it. I found our mother."

Allan smiled. "That is wonderful. So you met her."

"No, I talked with her on the phone and she's coming over tonight. Any minute now, actually. Oh, I wish Kerrian was here."

"I'll help you tidy up, then I'll leave."

"No, please stay. I don't know if I can do this by myself."

Allan nodded.

The knock on the door stunned both of them.

Lisa drew a sharp breath. "She's here? How do I look?"

"Very nice. I'll finish clearing this mess up. Go get the door."

While Lisa got to the door, Allan rushed the chocolates to the kitchen trashcan. When he stepped into the entryway, he saw the two women just staring at each other across the threshold.

Finally, Lisa spoke, "Mom."

"Lisa," her mother said, tears forming in her eyes.

They fell into each other's embrace and stayed like that for a while before pulling away.

"I guess there is much to say. I am not sure I know where to begin," said her mother. "And who is this handsome young man?"

"Oh. This is Allan, a good friend. Allan Johnson, this is my mom, Vivian Conners."

Allan shook her hand. She seemed kind and genuine. "A woman of great faith."

Ms. Conners seemed pleased. "Please call me Vivian. And are you, Mr. Johnson? A man of great faith that is."

"I am, Vivian."

"That suits me fine."

"Allan and I go to the same church."

"Oh, you don't know how much hearing that means to me."

"What, mom?"

"That you have a good friend from church."

"I never stopped going. It's a refuge sometimes, but I don't really believe in everything concerning the Christian faith."

"Well, I'm glad to know that you're well on your way."

Lisa nodded and fumbled awkwardly with the buttons on her blouse. "Would you like some coffee? Let's have some coffee. Mom, why don't you and Allan have a seat in the living room and I'll get busy in the kitchen."

Allen led Vivian to the living room and waited for her to sit before he took his seat.

"You're an Agent," she said, smiling at him.

Allan gulped. How did she know who he was?

She chuckled. "You should see your face right now. I've seen you in a vision."

"So, I've been outed." Allan leaned back against the soft cushions of the couch.

"No, not entirely. I haven't told Lisa, and I don't plan on telling anyone. You are here to help my Kerrian, aren't you?"

"Yes, ma'am."

"How can we help her?"

"Pray. Ms. Vivian, you can pray."

She pressed her lips into a resolute line and nodded. "When Lisa gets in here, we will do just that."

Vivian stood and walked to the fireplace. Pictures of Kerrian and Lisa were lined up along the mantelpiece. "I have made mistakes in the past. I gave my daughters up for adoption because I didn't have enough faith in the Provider. It took me a long while to acknowledge that. Then I spent ten years trying to locate them without luck, until now."

"I have learnt through all these years that there are some things we cannot fix...especially matters of the heart. This is a job for God alone."

She turned from the pictures of her daughters and looked him in the eye.

"I'm not trying to take over God's job. I'm just a representative, more like an earthly extension of God's hand. He uses me for His glory."

"Well, I just hope you know what you're doing getting involved in all this. If you truly believe that God is leading and directing your steps, then I will leave you be. But, be careful. Sometimes when human hands try to fix a mess, it only ends up being worse."

"I know."

"With that out of the way. Thank you."

They smiled at one another.

"I like you, Allan."

"And I like you, Vivian."

Lisa came in carrying a tray of coffee and sliced pound cake. "Good! We all like each other. Now we can get fat and happy together." She laughs. "If only Kerrian were here."

Her mother agreed with a nod. "Before we enjoy our coffee, can we pray together?"

Lisa looked uncomfortable. "I'm not that good at praying, mom."

Vivian sat on the couch beside her daughter. Allan enjoyed noticing the ways they favor one another. If only Kerrian were here.

"Praying is just talking with God, Lisa," Vivian said. "It's like a muscle, you know. The more you pray, the stronger you get."

Vivian placed a hand over her daughter's. "Oh sweet, Lisa. You don't know how many times I ached to hold your hands. Whenever I would see a mother holding her daughter's hand, my heart would break because I knew how much you probably wanted the same thing from me."

"I did, mom. But I forgive you. I told you that already on the phone."

Tears ran down Vivian's face. "I know. It's just hard for me to forgive myself."

"Will prayer help with that too, mom?"

Vivian smiled through the tears. "Well, look at you. Reminding me to take my own medicine."

They laughed together and then bowed their heads to pray. Allan bowed his head too but did not close his eyes. He took the vision card from his pocket and, sure enough, he saw Kerrian.

She was with Jason. He was in the cockpit of an airplane. It appeared to be a small area, maybe of a small plane. Kerrian had a drink in her hand, but she was crying. Her face was turned to the wall and her mouth was moving.

She was praying softly. At first, it was too low for Allan to hear, especially with Vivian praying on the living room sofa across the room. But, then he focused his heart on Kerrian's cry to God's heart and he heard her loud and clear.

"Lord, I know I haven't done this for so very long. I've made some huge mistakes in my life, but this one beats them all. I don't want to run away anymore. I don't want to leave like this, with this man I barely know and go to a foreign country. Leaving my family. I've been a bad choice of character in men again. Please,

God. Help me. Rescue me. Send an angel to bring me out of this mess."

Send an angel?

Allan stood up. "We've got to go to the airport right now."

The ladies sitting on the sofa looked at him in shock.

"Right now," Lisa asked. "What's going on?"

Lisa stayed seated, but her mother was already heading for the door. "Lisa, do as the man says. It's about Kerrian, isn't it?"

"Yes," he said, joining Vivian near the front door.

"But ..." Lisa protested.

"We'll take my car," Vivian offered. "I'm parked behind Lisa's car, I think."

Allan interrupted. "No, let's take mine."

"That old thing," Lisa protested. "It probably goes zero to 50 in five minutes." She laughed at her own joke. No one joined her.

Vivian looked at Allan. "Yes, let's take your car, young man."

"What?" Lisa asked. "But why are we going right this minute? I don't understand. How does this have anything to do with Kerrian?"

While Lisa peppered him with questions, Vivian leaned closer to Allan and whispered to him. "Do what you have to do to make sure we get to the airport in time to save her. Even if it means we will not remember any of it."

And with that invitation, Allan did what he was trained to do. Within seconds, they were at the airport he had seen in the vision card. But he had no way of knowing where Jason and Kerrian were. Or even when their plane was leaving.

The only thing he knew was Kerrian had prayed. And that's all he needed to know.

"You need help, Agent Johnson," Allan told himself. "Don't let your pride keep you from sending out a lifeline."

He pulled the communicator from his pocket and took a long breath. The ladies were still in the sleep state that he had put them in before transporting them here. They would be coming around any time.

It was now or never. He pressed the sequence of buttons on the communicator and waited.

Martin and Kaliel appeared beside the car.

"Hello, Agent Johnson," said Special Agent Martin.

"Good call, Sparky," Kaliel said. "As soon as you summoned us, a legion of other agents were dispersed in the area. We'll find them."

Lisa and her mother were stirring in the back seat.

"Take these ladies into the terminal. Get them a cup of coffee and something to eat. It might take a while. Jason Jones has been a hard one to catch. He won't give up without a fight."

"What about Kerrian?" Allan asked.

"Don't worry, she'll be fine," Martin said. "We'll bring her to you. Safe and sound. Safe and sound."

"She prayed for an angel."

"Yes, she did," Kaliel patted Allan on the shoulder. "You're her angel."

"Vivian knows who I am. And I guess Lisa will have to know too."

Kaliel shrugged. "That's the only way you can explain how you got them to Dulles in the blink of an eye. Take them to the café in Terminal B. We'll conceal your car. Good work, Johnson."

"Yeah, real good work. Real good work."

Chapter 5

Coffee and donuts were waiting for them in a corner booth. Allan waited patiently for the women to awake. He used the quiet time to compose his thoughts.

How was he going to explain all this to Lisa? It had to be the truth and nothing but the truth. And it had to be done gently.

"Where are we?" Lisa said as she wiped the sleep from her eyes. She looked down at the cup of coffee on the table in front of her. "We were going to go to the airport."

Her voice trailed off as she took in her surroundings.

Vivian gave Allan a sympathetic look. "Good luck explaining this one, young man."

"Wait a minute," Lisa exclaimed. "I've been here before. This is Dulles International Airport. Dulles! Oh my goodness."

Allan grimaced. "Shh."

She checked the time on her phone. "Five minutes ago we were sitting in my sister's living room, praying. How in the world could we travel hundreds of miles in five minutes? Am I dreaming?"

"Lisa, quiet down. You're causing a scene."

She looked Allan in the eye. "This isn't a dream, is it? I've been abducted. You're an alien."

"Lisa, do I really look like an alien."

She answered slowly. "No, you look like a fine looking young man to me."

Allan straightened his collar and smoothed his shirt over his chest.

Fine looking.

Vivian poked an elbow in his rib. "Pride goes before the fall, remember."

"Yes, ma'am."

"Tell her the truth."

Allan took a breath. Vivian was right.

"The truth is ..."

Allan stalled. He couldn't do it. He just couldn't do it. She'd laugh in his face.

"He's an angel, dear," Vivian said and took a sip of coffee. "Mmm. Good java."

Lisa's jaw went slack. "He's a what!"

Allan sighed. This was just the reaction he was trying to avoid. "I am an angel. An Agent of Christ to be more exact."

He waited for Lisa to respond. She just sat there staring. He wasn't even sure she was breathing.

"Lisa. Lisa. Are you okay? Say something."

"You're an angel?"

Vivian had pulled up a Bible app on her smart phone. She started to read out loud, "Be not forgetful to entertain strangers: for thereby some have entertained angels unawares. Hebrews chapter 13 verse 2." She took another sip of her coffee. "We're entertaining an angel. With coffee and donuts. I like that." She laughed.

"Mom, this is crazy." Lisa was still staring at him. In fact, she had leaned forward and looked at him closer. He was beginning to feel like a bug under a glass.

"Lisa, I can explain," he offered. "I am a specially trained ministering angel. I was assigned to help bring your sister home to a place of faith. This is actually my first case."

"First case?" Vivian asked. "Could have fooled me, young man."

"Thanks for saying that, Vivian. I needed that confidence boost."

"Angels need confidence boosts?" Lisa asked.

Allan shrugged. "I have weaknesses, too."

"So you were sent to help Kerry? If you could whisk us away to Dulles in the blink of an eye, why couldn't you just sprinkle some angel dust on my sister and make her do right?"

"It doesn't work that way, Lisa. She needed to make the choice for herself. She needed to pray for her deliverance. To ask for help."

"And did she?" Lisa asked.

Allan nodded. "While you and your mother were praying in Kerrian's living room. When you pray, in faith, for the person I'm assigned to, I have a way of seeing into the future."

"Into the future? This is a little hard to believe."

"I know it is. Prayer is the key to the work of the Agents. We can't effectively do our jobs without it. I'll bet you prayed to find your mother."

"Maybe I did say a little prayer."

"And, I prayed a lot," Vivian said.

"And, here we all are. Because of prayer."

Vivian nodded in full agreement as she devoured a donut. Lisa still looked doubtful.

"I have to admit, it's hard for me sometimes, this Christian faith thing. Yes, I go to church, but I'm a bit reserved in handing over my mind to someone I can't see."

Allan closed his eyes and thought about Lisa's words. "Do you believe in me?"

She picked up her coffee and blew across it before answering. "Of course I do. Okay, actually I think you're a little loopy after you just sat there and told me you're an angel and, mom, I'm worried about your mental state too, but I'm hoping this is one of my weird dreams. And I'm going to wake up at any minute."

What would help her believe he was an angel? Allan scratched his head. Then, it dawned on him that belief in the Agents of Christ didn't really matter as much as belief in the Christ.

"Lisa, it doesn't matter if you believe in me or not. Believe in the One who sent me."

"Maybe if we've really gotten this far with my sister, God is working it out after all."

Allan smiles.

"Don't get any ideas, Allan."

"Yeah, well, I'm praying for you too.

"I'm kinda glad you're here in my dream and that mom is here too."

Mom looked up briefly from her phone and smiled at her daughter. Vivian was playing Candy Crush.

"Finally, meeting my mother has been overwhelming but so very good. If only Kerrian was here. I wish that there was a way to prepare Kerrian to meet mom. I haven't said anything to Kerrian.

I don't know how she is going to react to all this. I think some form of preparation will be necessary."

Vivian responded without stopping her game. "I have been praying about that very thing, Lisa. If you pray, don't worry. If you worry, don't pray."

"Is that in the Bible too, mom?"

"Naw, just some cute saying somebody made up." Vivian pushed her phone aside and took her daughter's hands in hers. "I love you more than you can imagine. But, honey, I think you've got too much faith in yourself and your own abilities and not enough in the Almighty. Believing in God takes faith. Faith helps you *see* the things that are spiritual even when you can't see them with your eyes or understand them with your mind. Like our friend, Allan Johnson here."

The door to the café opened and Allan saw Kerrian walking toward them. Her eyes were cast to the ground. She seemed unsteady on her foot.

Lisa jumped to her feet. "Kerry."

Kerrian and Lisa embraced. Vivian stood to her feet too but seemed weak and nervous.

Allan touched Vivian's shoulder. "Are you okay?"

"I'll be okay. I've been praying for this moment for years. Praying for the return of my Prodigal Daughter. Now that the Lord has brought it to pass, I am overwhelmed with joy. God is so good. Give me a moment alone to just watch them."

"Sure." Allan walked closer to Kerrian and Lisa.

He heard Kerrian whispering to her sister. "I don't know how this happened, Lisa. One minute I was with Jason, having fun, then the next I realized this wasn't the way I should be living my life. It was like a light came on in my head and I knew how to find peace. I prayed, Lisa, for the first time in years."

"Kerry, that's wonderful." She paused and looked over her shoulder to where their mom was standing. "There's something I need to tell you."

Kerrian nodded.

"Mom is here. I don't know if this is a wacky dream or this is real. At any rate, she's over there, standing next to that table."

Within moments, Kerrian eyes welled with tears.

She took a shaky step toward her mother. "Mom?"

"Hi."

"Where have ... where have you been?"

"I've been away too long."

The distance closed until mother and daughter were wrapped in a long, tight embrace.

Kerrian spoke first. "For years, I've thought about some real nasty things to say to you if I ever saw you again. I wanted to hate you for abandoning us. I blamed you for everything that has ever gone wrong in my life."

"I know, and I don't blame you."

"I love you, mom. I'm still gonna give you a piece of my mind, but not today. Not today."

Lisa came into the embrace of mother and daughters reunited at last.

"Kerry, Lisa," Vivian said. "For years, I've searched for you relentlessly. I prayed that God would somehow reunite us again once more. I have been given that privilege and I want this moment to last forever."

"Me too, mom," Lisa said.

Allan was overwhelmed by the reunion. He could not hold his praise any longer. "Praise the Lord," he shouted.

"Amen, son. I'll be praising the Lord for a very long time too, that's for sure."

Allan walked closer, choking back tears. "Amen."

"I'll be seeing you at church."

"Yeah?"

"Yes. You were right, you know. God does have a way of working things out."

Lisa released her sister and mother and turned to face Allan. Despite her tears, she was smiling ear to ear. Allan hoped that now she would be convinced that this was not an elaborate dream.

"Now do you believe, Lisa?" he asked.

Without warning, she reached for him and pulled him into a tight embrace. For a split second, he went weak in the knees. He realized he had never been touched like this. He had touched humans, of course, but never on this deep level.

He saw straight into the center of her soul and he wondered if she could see him in that way. Of course, she couldn't, he reminded himself, *she* wasn't an Agent of Christ.

With her arms around him, he instantly knew all the questions she ever had about God and faith. He felt her longing for answers, for purpose in life. Using his powers, he probed deeper into her soul.

At that moment, he felt the presence of Light around him. He knew it was his fellow agents Martin and Kaliel.

"Be careful, Young Blood," Kaliel whispered to Allan.

"She's only human," Martin added. "Only human."

"Remember your purpose, Johnson," they said together and left just as quickly as they had come.

He felt Lisa take a sharp breath and step away from him. "Who are you?"

Uh oh.

So she had felt something when they hugged.

"I am an Agent of Christ." In that instant, he knew that she would be his next assignment. He smiled. "I am your friend, your servant."

She gave him an odd smile. "I think I see that now."

He was satisfied with her answer. This case had not gone as he had imagined it would, but the job was done.

"I must leave now. But I will return. The prodigal daughter has returned home. Case closed."

Personal Reflection

Journaling and personal reflection are very good practices to develop early in life. These stories weren't written just to entertain but to provoke thought and introspection, with the hope of helping readers make better choices in life and walk by faith. Get a journal and answer these questions as you reflect on the story you just read.

Life is filled with trauma, and many struggle to deal with the realities of life. Portraying an abusive husband who is possibly a pedophile may seem excessive, but this is loosely based on a true story. The struggle is real. Ler's see what we can get from this story during this time of reflection.

1. Should a woman remain in an abusive marriage? Give reasons for your answer.
2. Why do you think God allows us to go through pain and suffering? In answering this question, we can consider what Paul said: That these "light" afflictions cannot compare to the glory that will be revealed in us.
3. Do you think God knows or feels our pain?
4. What are some of the trauma and pain that you have gone through or are going through in your life?
5. Would you forgive your mom or dad for abandoning

you as child? Give reasons for your answer.

6. What does the Bible mean when it says we should be careful how we entertain strangers because they could be angels?

7. As believers, how can we emulate the role that Allan played in helping the Prodigal Daughter to return home?

Coming Soon

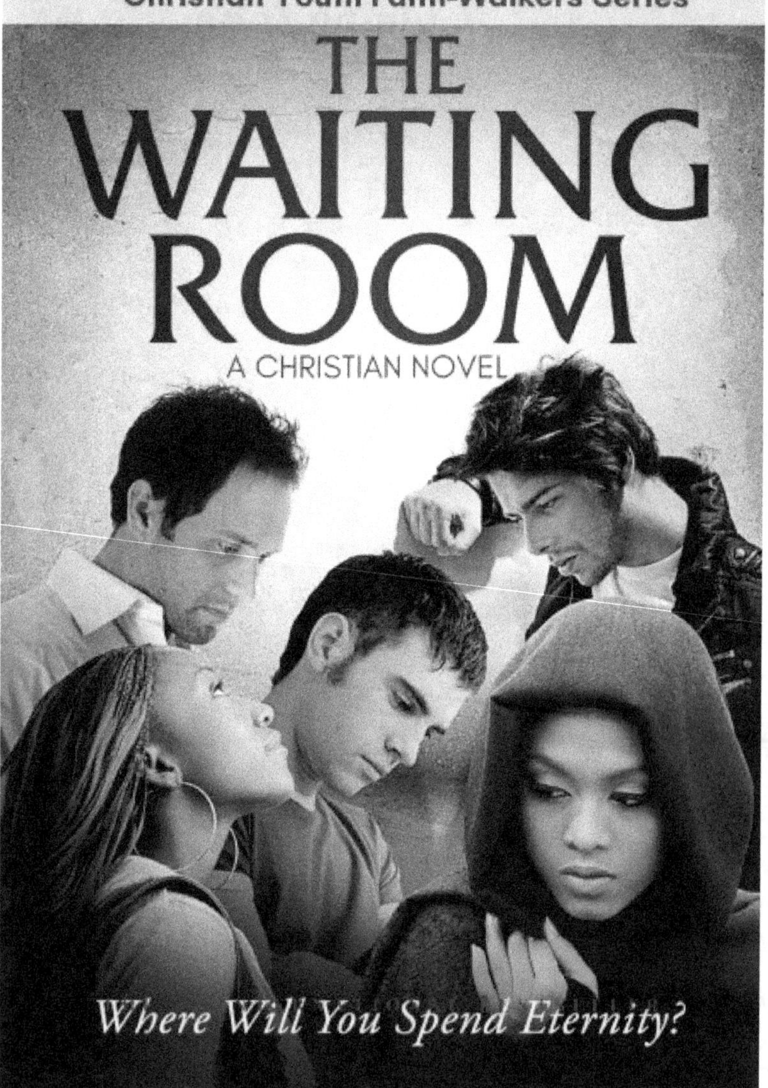

C. ORVILLE MCLEISH
Christian Youth Faith-Walkers Series
THE
WAITING
ROOM
A CHRISTIAN NOVEL
Where Will You Spend Eternity?

AGENTS OF CHRIST: THE PRODIGAL DAUGHTER: A CHRISTIAN NOVEL

49

C.ORVILLE MCLEISH

Preorder Available

50

FAITH
A THEOLOGICAL MEMOIR

Don't miss out!

Visit the website below and you can sign up to receive emails whenever C.Orville McLeish publishes a new book. There's no charge and no obligation.

https://books2read.com/r/B-A-GABRB-UBFQD

BOOKS 2 READ

Connecting independent readers to independent writers.

Did you love *Agents of Christ: The Prodigal Daughter: A Christian Novel*? Then you should read *Girl Unknown*[1] by C.Orville McLeish!

★★★★★ "It's been a long time since I couldn't put a book down. This is one I will think about for a long time." - Amazon Reviewer

Meet Chloe Cleopatra Taylor, a young woman whose haunted past casts a dark shadow over her present. Her life is filled with relentless challenges—balancing her career, navigating her mother's battle with addiction, and seeking her place in the world—Chloe's path takes an unexpected turn when

---

1. https://books2read.com/u/311zEW

2. https://books2read.com/u/311zEW

unexplainable events begin to unfold around her.Soon, the boundary between reality and the ethereal blur, and Chloe finds herself in a world where dreams and truths intertwine. Memories once forgotten surge to the surface from the depths of her mind, and she needs answers. In her pursuit of answers, Chloe is driven to peel away the layers of her father's history, setting off a chain reaction that will shatter the very foundation of her existence.Her father's death is a mystery that threatens everything Chloe cherishes. Her world is thrust into chaos as she confronts her inner demons and the truths she has long avoided. She discovers a connection between her and her mother that defies comprehension. The deeper she digs, the more mysterious her journey becomes threatening the very world she has created for herself. Chloe is gifted and poised to change the world, but her journey will reveal a truth about her that may take it all away.

Read more at https://clevelandomcleish.com/.

Also by C.Orville McLeish

Christian Youth Faith-Walkers Series
Detour: A Christian Novel
The Preacha And The Prostitute: A Christian Novel
Agents of Christ: The Prodigal Daughter: A Christian Novel

The Unshakable Series
FAITH: A Theological Memoir

Standalone
Girl Unknown
Who I Am In Christ Daily Devotionals
How to Receive Your Healing
Sons of God: A Study on the Biblical Narrative of the Sons of
God
Made in God's Image: We are Partakers of God's Divine Nature

Watch for more at https://clevelandomcleish.com/.

About the Author

C. Orville McLeish is a successful entrepreneur, and an acclaimed multi-award-winning author, playwright, and screenwriter. He is a professional ghostwriter, copy editor and self-publishing service provider. With a deep commitment to intellectual and mystical theology, he intertwines his passion for health, fitness, longevity, and Christian spirituality. A proud graduate of Writer's Digest University and the School of Kingdom Ministries, Cleveland is currently pursuing a master's in theological studies at Gordon-Conwell Theological Seminary.

Read more at https://clevelandomcleish.com/.